Dear Parent:
Your child's love of reading starts here!

Every child learns to read in a different way and at his or her own speed. Some go back and forth between reading levels and read favorite books again and again. Others read through each level in order. You can help your young reader improve and become more confident by encouraging his or her own interests and abilities. From books your child reads with you to the first books he or she reads alone, there are I Can Read Books for every stage of reading:

SHARED READING
Basic language, word repetition, and whimsical illustrations, ideal for sharing with your emergent reader

BEGINNING READING
Short sentences, familiar words, and simple concepts for children eager to read on their own

READING WITH HELP
Engaging stories, longer sentences, and language play for developing readers

READING ALONE
Complex plots, challenging vocabulary, and high-interest topics for the independent reader

ADVANCED READING
Short paragraphs, chapters, and exciting themes for the perfect bridge to chapter books

I Can Read Books have introduced children to the joy of reading since 1957. Featuring award-winning authors and illustrators and a fabulous cast of beloved characters, I Can Read Books set the standard for beginning readers.

A lifetime of discovery begins with the magical words "I Can Read!"

Visit www.icanread.com for information
on enriching your child's reading experience.

I Can Read Book® is a trademark of HarperCollins Publishers.

Mia and the Dance for Two
Copyright © 2011 by HarperCollins Publishers
All rights reserved. Manufactured in the United States of America.
www.icanread.com

Library of Congress Cataloging-in-Publication Data is available.
ISBN 978-0-06-173304-8 (trade bdg.) —ISBN 978-0-06-173303-1 (pbk.)

Design by Sean Boggs

13   14   15   LP/WOR   10   9   8   7   6   5   4   3   ❖   First Edition

I Can Read!™ SHARED My First READING

Mia
and the Dance for Two

by Robin Farley
Pictures by Aleksey and Olga Ivanov

HARPER

An Imprint of HarperCollinsPublishers

Today in class,
Mia is going to learn a dance
for two.

She is going to dance
with her best friend, Ruby!

Mia slips on her slippers.
She is ready to dance.

"Where is Ruby?"

Mia wonders.

She waits and waits.

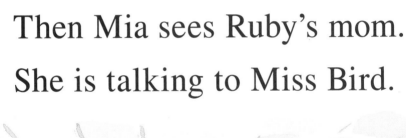

Then Mia sees Ruby's mom.
She is talking to Miss Bird.

Ruby is sick.

Ruby will not dance today.

"All dancers
on the dance floor!"
sings Miss Bird.

Mia does not have
a partner for the dance
for two.

Mia feels very lonely.

Mia feels a tap, tap, tap.
"Will you be my partner?"
asks Bella.

Mia feels a pat, pat, pat.
"Will you be my partner?"
asks Ali.

Mia looks at Bella.

She looks at Ali.

Now Mia has too many
partners for the dance
for two!

Miss Bird starts class.
"One, two, three, four,"
she counts.

Mia knows how it feels
to be alone.

She does not want her
friends to feel lonely.

Mia's eyes sparkle.
She whispers to her teacher.

"A fine idea!"
sings Miss Bird.

"Will you be my partner?"
Mia asks Bella.

"Will you be my partner?"
Mia asks Ali.

Mia takes her friends
by the hands.

"Let's dance!" she tells them.

The friends spring
to their toes!

They twirl around
and around!

The three friends are happy
dancing the dance for two!

"Bravo!" sings Miss Bird.

Dictionary

Miss Bird's School of Dance

First Position

Stand with your heels together and your toes pointed outward, forming a straight line.

Second Position

Stand with your toes pointed outward and your heels a foot apart

Third Position

Stand with one foot in front of the other so the heel of the front foot touches the middle of the back foot.

Fourth Position

Start in Third Position and take a small step forward with your front foot.

Fifth Position

Stand with one foot in front of the other so the heel of each foot touches the toes of the other foot.